Sparky
at
Magic School

WITHDRAWN

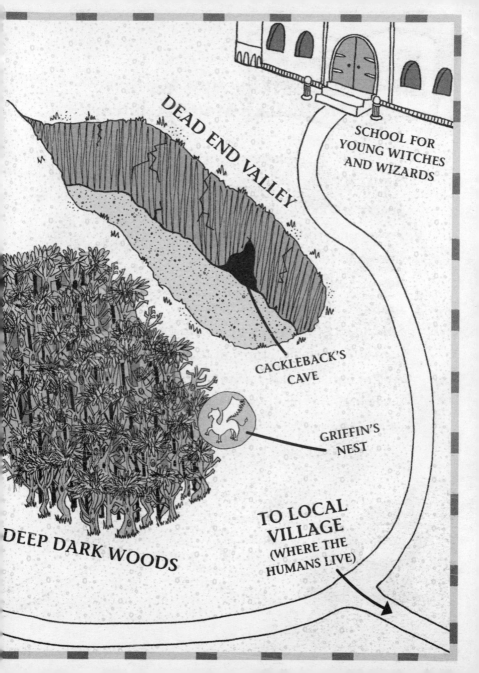

SCHOOL FOR
YOUNG WITCHES
AND WIZARDS

DEAD END VALLEY

CACKLEBACK'S
CAVE

GRIFFIN'S
NEST

DEEP DARK WOODS

TO LOCAL
VILLAGE
(WHERE THE
HUMANS LIVE)

Meet the stars of
Mrs Mothwick's Magic Academy!

Sparky

Sparky is a fluffy, bouncy puppy with brown and white splodges. He has always lived at the Green Meadow Rescue Centre with lots of other animals, including his best friend, Sox. Sparky dreams about having an owner to tickle his tummy and a bowl (full of marshmallows) with his name on it. He is adventurous and playful, so when he ends up at Mrs Mothwick's Magic Academy, he can't help getting into trouble!

Sox

Sox is Sparky's best friend. She is a sensible kitten with jet-black fur and white paws. She loves Sparky and does her best to keep him out of mischief.

Trixie

Trixie is a sleek black cat. She's very good at magic but is a bit of a bully. She doesn't like dogs, so Sparky had better watch out!

Mrs Mothwick

Mrs Mothwick is head of the Magic Academy. She has a thin, warty face and wears a tall black hat. Her familiar – her special animal friend with whom she has a magical bond – is a gruff vulture called Mr Carrion. She is proud of her Magic Academy, but she worries that her son, Carl, isn't ready to be a wizard.

Carl Mothwick

Carl is a bit clumsy and scruffy. His shoelaces always seem to be untied, and he smells of mud and chewing gum. Even though he tries really hard, poor Carl just isn't very good at magic. He never knows where his wand is and even when he does find it, he can't make it work the way the other trainees can. Carl is desperate to prove to everyone, including his mum, that he is a proper wizard like his dad.

Mrs Cackleback

Mrs Cackleback is the only witch ever to own a terrifying griffin as her familiar, but the less said about her and her wicked ways, the better . . .

Sparky
at
Magic School

RUBY NASH

Illustrated by Clare Elsom

RED FOX

SPARKY AT MAGIC SCHOOL
A RED FOX BOOK 978 1 782 95298 5

First published in Great Britain by Red Fox,
an imprint of Random House Children's Publishers UK
A Random House Group Company

This edition published 2014

1 3 5 7 9 10 8 6 4 2

Series created by Working Partners Limited
Copyright © Working Partners Limited, 2014
Cover and interior illustrations copyright © Clare Elsom, 2014
With special thanks to Pip Jones

The Random House Group Limited supports the Forest Stewardship
Council® (FSC®), the leading international forest-certification organisation.
Our books carrying the FSC label are printed on FSC®-certified paper.
FSC is the only forest-certification scheme supported by the leading
environmental organisations, including Greenpeace.
Our paper procurement policy can be found at
www.randomhouse.co.uk/environment

MIX
Paper from
responsible sources
FSC® C016897

Set in ITC Stone Informal

Red Fox Books are published by Random House Children's Publishers UK,
61–63 Uxbridge Road, London W5 5SA

www.randomhousechildrens.co.uk
www.totallyrandombooks.co.uk
www.randomhouse.co.uk

Addresses for companies within The Random House Group Limited can be
found at: www.randomhouse.co.uk/offices.htm

THE RANDOM HOUSE GROUP Limited Reg. No. 954009

A CIP catalogue record for this book is available from the British Library.

Printed and bound in Great Britain by
CPI Group (UK) Ltd, Croydon CR0 4YY

Turn to page 177 for lots of magical activities!

MRS MOTHWICK'S MAGIC ACADEMY

1

Whoosh!

Sparky's eyes popped open. He
sat up with a noisy "Yip!"

"What was that?" It wasn't the
soft mewing noise that Cheshire, the
three-legged tabby cat, made when

he was dreaming. It wasn't the clanging clatter of breakfast bowls that meant morning was close.

Sparky knew all the noises at Green Meadow Rescue Centre. He had lived there since he was a tiny puppy, hoping that an owner would one day come and choose him. This was a new sound.

"Sox?" Sparky yelped. "Did you hear it, too?"

"Yes!" a little voice said from the darkness.

Sparky peered through the bars towards his friend's cage in the gloom. "I can't see you," he whispered.

The kitten was as black as night, apart from four perfectly white paws. She stuck a front foot through the bars and wiggled it.

"That's better!" said Sparky. "What do you think it was?"

Before Sox could reply, the noise
came again – a **whoosh**.

"Let's go and see!" Sparky said.
The door to his cage was kept shut
by a hook, but he really wanted to
get out. As he wriggled his snout
between the bars, a faraway clock
began to chime.

Bong. Bong. Bong.

If he could just get the cage
open . . . Sparky counted the chimes

as he balanced the end of the
hook on his nose. **Four, five, six,
seven . . .** He gave an extra wriggly
wriggle of his nose and pushed
it upwards. **Eight, nine, ten,
eleven . . .**

The clock struck twelve. The
hook popped free and the door
swung open. He'd done it!

Sparky scampered over to Sox's
cage. "Your turn now," he said.

Opening her door was much

easier. Sparky flicked his paw and
the hook lifted. Sox gave a little
purr and pushed her way out.

"Let's see if—" Sox stopped talking at the sound of footsteps coming from outside. None of the other animals heard. Dogs snored softly. Cats and rabbits snoozed silently. Birds on perches hid their beaks under their wings.

A shadow loomed through the window.

"Quick!" Sox squealed.

They dived into her cage and buried themselves under her wool

blanket just as the back door creaked
open. Sparky stuck his nose out and
gave a sniff. The air smelled of spice
and wood, and a strange scent that
made him feel tingly all over . . .

"Who is it?" Sox asked.

"Someone new," Sparky replied.

The footsteps were loud and close.
"Her name is Sox," came a woman's
voice. "Check the labels on the
cages."

"You must be getting an owner!"

Sparky whispered.

Having a human to call their own was what Sparky and Sox talked about most. They dreamed of collars, and tummy tickles, and bowls with their names on.

"But it's the middle of the night," said Sox. "Why would they come now?"

Peeping out from under the blanket, Sparky could see a pale, bony hand stretch towards them.

"Here she is. That's funny . . . the cage isn't shut." A thin, warty face peered in. Sparky could just make it out from where he was hidden.

"Ah, Sox. There's a good kitty. Come along with Mrs Mothwick!"

The hand closed the cage door and flipped back the hook, shutting the little animals inside. A somersault feeling in Sparky's tummy told him the cage had been lifted, and he caught a glimpse of two black boots. A long skirt swished around them, its twinkly purple and black frills rustling with each step.

Suddenly an icy gust of wind billowed from somewhere beneath the cage. Sparky shivered. Then there was another **whoosh**ing sound, just like the noise that had woken him.

"What's happening?" asked Sox, trembling.

Sparky shook his head free of the blanket. Hunched next to the cage was an enormous, ugly bird. Its neck was long and crooked, its head

bald and wrinkled. Its hooded eyes peered over a sharp, hooked beak. One of the bird's wings held the cage in place.

In front of the bird, Sparky could see the back of someone he assumed must be Mrs Mothwick. Her long hair streamed out from beneath a tall, pointy hat. To the left, almost close enough to touch, was a massive moonlit cloud. Sparky whimpered and pulled his

head under the blanket again. His
stomach flipped as they

looped
loop-the-

and whizzed through the air.

"We're flying on a broomstick!" he told Sox.

"What? How?" Sox whispered.

Sparky had seen pictures in books that children brought to the rescue centre, but he never thought they could be real. "Mrs Mothwick . . ." he stuttered.

"She's a witch!"

MRS MOTHWICK'S MAGIC ACADEMY

2

The witch's hair whipped in the wind
and the bird's feathers ruffled. Far
below, the trees looked tiny. They'd
been travelling all night and now
they were zooming over a group of
buildings hidden in the woods.

Sox opened one eye, then the other. "What's that?" she asked Sparky.

The largest building was huge, and the front was carved into the shape of a man's face. On each corner of the black roof were four

spiky spires. Stone serpents with
jewelled eyes curled down each one.
They seemed to be keeping watch.

The broomstick whizzed over a
wooden bridge and through the
open mouth of the building into a
courtyard set up with jumps, hoops

and a sandpit. It looked a bit like a
playground.

"It looks like a training school!"
Sparky cried. **"Wowzers!**
They teach pets things like sitting
and doing tricks."

"But why would anyone bring
me to a training school?" Sox asked.
"Cats don't do tricks."

"That's true," agreed Sparky. But
if this place wasn't a pet training
school, then what could it be?

Sparky and Sox dipped under
the blanket again. Suddenly the
broomstick came to an abrupt halt.
Sparky felt the cage being lifted. It
swung gently as the witch carried it
indoors.

When Sparky dared to look out
again, he discovered he was in a
room lined with bookshelves. The
air smelled musty and dusty. Sparky
flinched when the witch's face
appeared over the top of the cage.

"Sox!" came her loud, prim
voice. "I am Mrs Mothwick."

Beneath Mrs Mothwick's hat, her
thick dark hair was speckled with
silver. Sparky hoped she was a *good*
witch, but her face was stern and
her icy blue eyes looked serious.

"You were spotted by one of our
secret scouts, Sox," Mrs Mothwick
continued. "It seems you might
have the gift."

As she spoke, she reached into

the cage and whipped away the blanket. Her eyes grew wide as she looked from Sox to Sparky and back again. She bent down low, so that her large, knobbly nose almost touched Sparky's wet one.

"Who do we have here?"

Mrs Mothwick asked.

Sparky swallowed hard.

The ugly bird hopped over. "A stowaway, eh?" he squawked. "Your name?"

Sparky's legs felt really wobbly. "Sparky," he whimpered.

"Sparky," repeated Mrs Mothwick.

She could understand animals! He'd never met a person who could understand animals before. What

other powers might she have?

Mrs Mothwick reached into the cage and Sparky scrambled backwards, trying to get away. But her cool hand grasped the scruff of his neck as she pulled him out and plonked him down on the wooden floor. She placed Sox next to him.

Just then, a door crashed open
and a scruffy boy stumbled in,
tripping over his shoelace.

"Mum, you're back!" the boy
spluttered. His cheeks were flushed.
"I've lost my wand! I've looked
everywhere. I know I had it last
night, but I'm not sure where,
and—"

"Lost your wand again, Carl?"
Mrs Mothwick sighed. "For
goodness' sake."

Carl spotted Sparky, cowering next to his mum's feet. "A puppy!" he cried, scooping him up and giving him a massive cuddle.

Carl smelled of mud and chewing gum. He seemed just the sort of owner Sparky wanted. Sparky nuzzled

into his warm woolly jumper.

"Hi, Carl, I'm Sparky!" the puppy
said, squirming and trying to lick
Carl's nose. If Mrs Mothwick could
understand him, maybe Carl could
as well. But Carl just giggled and
tickled Sparky's chin.

The bird beat his huge wings.
"The last thing we need at this
school is an excitable puppy," he
grumbled.

"Mr Carrion's right," Mrs

Mothwick said as she tapped her
boot on the floor. "If an animal
isn't born with magic, it will never
become a familiar." She plucked
the puppy out of her son's arms.
"Sparky is going back to the rescue
centre."

"Aww!" Carl whined.

"But this kitten is perfect," his
mother said, bending to stroke Sox.

Sparky wriggled out of Mrs
Mothwick's arms and hid under the

desk. He didn't want to go back to
the rescue centre. He wanted to stay
with Sox.

Sparky saw Mrs Mothwick's boots
clip-clopping over to the desk. The
witch stooped down. "Come on,
puppy," she said, holding out her
hand.

But Sparky was distracted by the
smell of mud and chewing gum
. . . and also wood. A stick? Would
Carl like a game of fetch? Sparky's

nose dropped to the floor. The stick
was behind the furthest leg of the
desk. When Sparky picked it up, he
couldn't help but gnaw at the wood
a little. He dragged it out to show
Carl, but Mr Carrion blocked his
path.

"Shoo!"

said the vulture gruffly. His wings opened, like great black curtains.

"Wait!" Carl cried. "He's found my wand!"

Mrs Mothwick bent down and took the wand out of Sparky's mouth. She turned it in her hand, and tutted when she saw it was bent and chewed.

"Thanks, Sparky!" Carl said.

"Can't we let him have a go at the
school, Mum? Please?"

Sparky really wanted to stay. He
sat, like a good dog.

Mrs Mothwick stood with her
arms folded, a single long nail
tapping against her arm. "I don't
know . . . It goes against all the
rules set by the GRAND COUNCIL OF
WIZARDRY AND WITCHINESS." Then
she gave a deep sigh. "OK. But one
mistake and back he goes to the

humans at the rescue centre."

"Hooray!" shouted Carl.

I may not have any magic, Sparky thought, *but I'll be the best behaved puppy ever.*

He yipped with joy, earning him a frown from Mr Carrion.

Sparky sat up neatly. *Starting from now.*

3

Sparky shook his head and tried to blink the sleepiness away. He had never been awake for a whole night before.

The Dining Hall was bustling with hungry animals. On a long

perch, a group of chicks fidgeted
beside a much larger tawny owl.
Two rats were tickling the curly tail
of a piglet in front of them. There
were crows, squirrels and cats. There
was even a frog, which leaped over
Sparky's head and gave a loud

Ribbet!

There were no other dogs,
though.

In front of all the animals were
plates, troughs, dishes and bowls.
"Look," Sparky said excitedly. "The
bowls have *names on*!"

Sox found her bowl. There was
one next to it, but it was just plain
with no writing.

"That must be yours," she
said. "Just for now . . ." she added
soothingly.

Sparky felt sad. He was the
only one without a special bowl.
To make it worse, he could hear
someone sniggering.

A glossy, jet-black kitten turned
round to face Sparky. "A puppy!"
she sneered. "And with that fur! Is it
brown? Is it white?"

"Well,
I—"
Sparky
began,

but the kitten carried on talking.

"It's all mixed up and messy!"
She leaned towards three mice who
were sitting next to her and said,
just loudly enough for Sparky to
hear, "Puppies are never magical.
He's bound to bring down the good
name of the school."

The kitten sighed as if she felt
sorry for Sparky. "I'm Trixie,"
she purred. "One of seventeen
generations of familiars. Unlike *you*,

I imagine." Her eyes fixed on Sox.
"What *are* those, anyway?" she
asked with a sniff, waving her tail
at Sox's white feet.

"My paws?" Sox replied.

"Oh!" Trixie tittered. "I thought
you'd walked through
a bag of flour!"

The three
white mice
burst into fits of
squeaky giggles.

"Harry, Larry, Sid," Trixie snapped, "be quiet."

The mice stopped instantly.

Something tapped Sparky on the back of the head. He turned to see a cloth sack, floating in mid-air.

"How is it doing that?" he asked.

A ladle hovered out of the sack and spooned something into his bowl. It was a disgusting mixture that wobbled like jelly, and glowed bright red like the hot coals of a

fire. Another dollop splatted in Sox's dish, then the ladle continued down the line.

"I don't know if I can eat this," Sparky whimpered. They watched the other animals begin eating. As a squirrel prepared to take a bite, there was a **puff** of glitter around his bowl and the horrible gooey jelly turned into acorns!

"Did you see that?" Sox yelped. Sparky and Sox looked at their

own bowls. **Puff!** White fish for
Sox. **Puff!** Biscuits for Sparky.

The food was magic! When Sparky took his first gulp, he found blobs of sweetness mixed in. "This is amazing," he woofed to Sox with his mouth full. "Mine has even got marshmallows in it – my favourite!"

This was just the first morning in the training school – he couldn't imagine what the rest of the day would bring.

Morning light poured through
the huge stained-glass windows of
the Great Hall, throwing dazzling
colours onto the polished floor.
On one window was a picture

of a woman holding a ball of fire.
Another showed a coiled-up snake
cradling a baby. Hanging on the
wall was a massive painting of a
man with wiry grey hair. His face

looked like the one carved into
the building. A long green snake
with red eyes was draped over his
shoulders.

Dangling down from the ceiling
were green banners, with words
written in gold, swirly writing.

The animals had been led from
the Dining Hall to the Grand
Hall. At the front of the room, Mrs
Mothwick was watching.

"Sit!" she ordered. All the

animals sat down at once.

"Welcome to the Beginners' Class for Familiars. Let's start with our school motto." Mrs Mothwick pointed a bony finger at a banner hanging behind her, and read:

"Hand, fur
and feather,
Magic friends
for ever."

The class repeated the lines in squeaks and chirrups.

"It means," Mrs Mothwick bellowed, *"I will always be completely and totally loyal to my owner.* It's the most important thing a familiar must learn."

There's that strange word again, Sparky thought. "What's a familiar?" he asked Sox in a whisper.

"The dog doesn't even know what a familiar is!" laughed Trixie, who

was sitting right behind Sparky.

Sparky could feel his ears growing prickly with embarrassment.

Mrs Mothwick clapped her hands. "Enter, witches and wizards!" she yelled.

A door opened and a line of boys and girls filed in. They stood behind Mrs Mothwick, facing the animals. When Sparky saw Carl at the end of the line, he gave a little yip.

Carl spotted him and waved. Sparky wagged his tail even harder, beating the wooden floor. Trixie tutted.

Mrs Mothwick held up her hand to quieten the room. "Today is an important day," she said. "Today the young witches and wizards in training have come from their school to choose their familiars."

A young rabbit drummed his foot on the floor, annoying the red-eyed rat next to him.

Mrs Mothwick continued.
"A witch is not a witch without
a familiar – a magical animal
friend," she said, pacing before the
class. "And a familiar is not
a familiar without a witch –

or a wizard, of course."

Suddenly Sparky realized. *All the animals here are familiars. And if I can be a familiar, a witch or wizard might choose me.* He felt as if his fur was standing on end.

He and Sox shared a look. He knew exactly what his friend was thinking. They had spent months at the Green Meadow Rescue Centre, waiting and hoping for this moment. *I'll have an owner!*

Mrs Mothwick looked around at the animals. "Most of you are well on your way to learning how to do magic." Her eyes fixed on Sox. "Those of you who aren't will have to work *very hard* to catch up. That's if you have the ability to do magic at all," the witch added. Now she was looking sternly at Sparky. "Some of you may not."

Sparky's heart sank. *Familiars are supposed to be magical,* he thought.

I'm not magical.

He knew what that meant.

None of the trainees will pick me.

Sparky had never been so close
to having his dreams come true.
Now it seemed they never would.

MRS MOTHWICK'S MAGIC ACADEMY

4

Sparky's heart was thumping. He watched as the trainees took their wands out of their pockets.

"Witches and wizards," Mrs Mothwick said loudly, "if you have practised, your magic will choose

the best familiar for you. Trainees
and familiars with a strong magical
bond will be able to understand
each other straight away."

Sparky fidgeted. He didn't have a
magical *anything*.

Mrs Mothwick continued.
"Eventually your familiar will
learn to speak to all witches and
wizards, like Mr Carrion does."

Mr Carrion was snoozing and
he snorted in his sleep, making

some of the familiars giggle. Mrs
Mothwick cleared her throat loudly,
then said, "So, let's have good,
strong magical leads."

"I hope you get someone nice,
Sox," Sparky whispered.

"You too," Sox replied and curled
her tail round Sparky's for luck.

Mrs Mothwick beckoned to a
girl with long black hair and big
green eyes. "Would you care to
demonstrate, Amelia?"

Amelia stepped forward, beaming.
She made two small circles in
the air with her wand, then
flicked it sharply.

Whizz! A shimmering golden cord shot out from the end of Amelia's wand and twirled through the air towards the animals. It zoomed over Sparky's head and looped itself neatly around Trixie's neck, like a collar and lead.

With a **puff!** the lead vanished and golden glitter hung in the air. The collar glowed gently around Trixie's neck, making her eyes shine. She pranced towards Amelia.

"I knew I'd get the best witch!" the kitten purred, circling the girl's legs.

"And I knew I'd get the best familiar!" Amelia replied. The animals muttered and nudged each other – Amelia could understand Trixie perfectly!

"Wowzers!" Carl exclaimed. "They did it first time."

Mrs Mothwick turned to the other boys and girls. "Now the rest of you may try," she said.

The trainees stood side by side,
holding their wands in front of
them. The animals gasped as
magical leads came darting out.

The Great Hall glittered with shimmering twirls of light. Harry, Larry and Sid squeaked excitedly as they spotted the leads of three small, identical boys.

"It's the triplets!" Larry squealed.

"Me first, me first!" All three mice
jumped to get a lead, then landed
in a heap on the floor, just as the
magical leads found them.

Sparky and Sox couldn't help
but giggle.

Bats were colliding mid-air, rats were scrambling across the floor. All around there were **puffs** and **flashes**, **squeaks** and **squawks**. Suddenly a magical lead zoomed past Sparky and looped around Sox's neck.

"I got one!" Sox cried.

The lead belonged to a girl with a white stripe in her hair. "Hi!" she said cheerfully to Sox. "I'm Sophie. I like your paws."

"I'm Sox!" the kitten replied,
bounding over to meet her new
witch. "I like your hair."

"Thanks," Sophie replied.

Sophie could understand her! Sparky smiled. **"Wowzers!** You did it, Sox!"

Sox gave a happy, high-pitched **"Prrr!"**

There were only one or two more trainees left. Carl was one of them. He kept flicking his wand, but no magical lead was coming out. Sparky could see that the wood was still bent and chewed from when he'd found it.

Oh no, he thought. *I broke his wand.*

Sparky's ears pricked when he heard someone saying Carl's name.

"It's hard to believe Carl's a Mothwick," Amelia whispered to the other trainees. "His parents founded the most famous familiar training school in the Magic World, but he's awful at magic! He hardly deserves a wand, let alone a familiar."

Carl glanced at Amelia. He looked hurt but said nothing.

Sparky growled.

"Maybe Mr Mothwick's not a proper wizard," Amelia continued, while her friends giggled.

"He *is* a proper wizard," Carl replied quietly, looking up at the portrait of the man with the wiry hair. "He's away on **important wizarding business**, collecting magical ingredients to protect our school."

Amelia rolled her eyes.

A boy with big round glasses and long teeth finally threw out a magical lead. It wound through the air like a wriggly snake, then plopped into a goldfish bowl.

"Well done, George," Mrs Mothwick said to the boy.

Under the water, the goldfish grinned. "I'm Gill!" he said in a bubbly voice. The rim of his bowl glowed magically.

Now Carl was the last trainee left
without a familiar. His face was red.
There were only a few animals for
him to choose from.

Sparky gave Carl an encouraging
"Yip!"

Carl saw Sparky. He shrugged
and put his wand down.

No, don't give up! Sparky thought
to himself, giving a growly whine.

Carl knelt down on the floor. He
grinned. "Come, Sparky!" he cried.

Me? Sparky barked happily and leaped into Carl's arms. "You were the one I wanted!" he told Carl, licking the boy's face.

Carl didn't understand what he was saying, but it didn't matter to Sparky. *He had an owner!*

"Wait!" called Mrs Mothwick, striding over to her son. "This is *not* how we do things, Carl. Trainees and familiars must be paired magically."

"But Mum!" Carl said. "I want
Sparky."

Sparky could have glowed in
delight.

Mr Carrion swooped down from
his perch. "It goes against the rules
of the school," the bird said coldly.
"And the rules of the GRAND COUNCIL
OF WIZARDRY AND WITCHINESS."

Carl looked pleadingly at his
mum, while Mr Carrion scowled.

"We'll try really hard, I promise."

Mrs Mothwick paused, then said:
"All right. Just on trial, remember."

Carl stroked Sparky's ears. "I
don't care what anyone thinks," he
whispered. "We'll be the best team
ever!"

The boy took a shoelace out
of his pocket and tied it in a bow
around Sparky's neck. "I know it's
not a magic, glowing collar, but it'll
have to do for now."

Sparky knew Carl wouldn't

understand him, so he raised a paw and rested it on his new friend's hand to let him know how very, *very* hard he was going to try.

5

Outside, the chilly breeze ruffled Sparky's fur, making him shiver. A pale sun peeped out from behind the dark clouds.

Sparky looked up. The face

carved into the building in front of him was enormous. Its eyes were fixed in a stony stare, gazing over the Courtyard. A high wall, covered in ivy, surrounded all the buildings. The jumps, hoops and sandpit Sparky had seen the night before from Mrs Mothwick's broomstick were behind a fountain shaped like five flying bats.

All the witches, wizards and familiars were standing in a circle.

Birds perched on shoulders, rats and squirrels nestled in hands, frogs poked out of pockets. A spider was sitting on the tip of his witch's nose, making her go cross-eyed. In the middle of the circle was Mrs Mothwick.

"Welcome to your first broomstick-flying lesson," she said. She bent down and placed

her broomstick by her feet, and Mr
Carrion hopped onto the back of it.
He flapped his black wings twice,
then folded them back into place.
**"A broomstick will not
fly without a familiar on
board,"** Mrs Mothwick explained.
"Now, everyone watch closely."

She held one hand high above
her broomstick. She wiggled
her bony fingers and the stick
floated smoothly up into the air.

Mr Carrion didn't wobble once.

When the broomstick was high enough, Mrs Mothwick sat on it. She flew in a neat circle around the fountain. "Now, you can all try," she said when she landed. "Don't fly any higher than the spires, and do *not* leave the school grounds. You might accidentally end up in the

Deep Dark Wood."

Some of the trainees muttered.
Mrs Mothwick shushed them. "The
Deep Dark Wood is full of
danger," she explained. "There are
grabby trees and **gulp pits**,
dragon's lairs and **troll's
traps**. There was even a **griffin**
spotted there once, a long time ago."

"What's a griffin?" Sparky
whispered to Sox.

Mrs Mothwick heard. "A griffin is
a fierce creature," she said gravely.

She whipped her hand through
the air and, with a **puff** of glitter,
a picture appeared. "It is half

lion, half eagle. Only one witch
in history has owned a griffin
familiar . . ." Mrs Mothwick trailed
off. "But the less said about her and
her wicked ways, the better."

Sparky gulped hard and
shuddered.

"Now, off you go," Mrs Mothwick
said. "Use your wands."

The witches and wizards put
their broomsticks on the ground.
Carl's rolled away and bumped

into Gill's bowl, making the water splash.

Sparky watched Trixie sit on Amelia's broomstick and twitch her whiskers. Amelia flicked her wand and the broomstick floated into the air. The girl climbed on.

"Easy peasy," said Trixie as Amelia steered in a perfect circle around the spires of the tall building.

"Come on, Sparky," Carl said

quietly. "We'll show them."

Sparky sat on the back of Carl's broomstick. Carl flicked his wand **once, twice, three** times . . . The broomstick jerked and then lifted wonkily into the air.

Sparky instantly slipped off.

"Sorry," Carl said. "Let's try again."

Sparky glanced around the Courtyard. Everyone was flying now: even Gill's bowl had hovered up neatly and sat on the end of George's broomstick.

Poor Carl, Sparky thought. *This is all my fault. If only I had some magic in me.*

"Perhaps I could help?" came a whisper.

Sparky turned to see Trixie.

Harry, Larry and Sid were behind her, chuckling.

"How?" Sparky asked warily.

"You see that bush with the stikwik berries?" Trixie waved her tail towards the plump black fruits. "Pick one. Squeeze the juice into the fountain, then dip your paws in."

Sparky wasn't sure he should.

"You don't want to make Carl look silly, do you?" Trixie asked sweetly.

Carl was inspecting his wand closely and no one else was looking, so Sparky did as Trixie told him. With tingling feet, he scampered back to Carl and carefully sat on the broomstick again.

Carl flicked his wand **once, twice, three** times . . .

"Silly wand," the boy mumbled.

He shrugged, then dropped the wand and picked up the broomstick with his hands. Sparky stayed on!

"You're doing it, Sparky," Carl cried. "Good dog!"

He climbed onto the front of the stick. "Here goes," he said shakily.

The broomstick jolted forwards, and with a sudden *whoosh!* they were in the air.

"Yip!" Sparky barked happily.

"We're flying!"

Sparky and Carl soared upwards, higher than the fountain. Carl tried to steer the broomstick but it jerked sharply left, then right.

"Concentrate!" Mrs Mothwick yelled to her son.

Sparky jumped at the sound of the witch's booming voice, making the broomstick wobble. Then the stick leaned, and leaned even further . . . then tipped upside down!

"Wah!" Carl cried. Sparky tried to scrabble with his feet to turn them the right way up, but his paws were stuck like glue. The broomstick

climbed higher and higher.

"Help!" called Carl. He was
dangling down, clinging to the stick
with his fingertips, trying not to fall.
"It's too fast, I can't stop it!"

"YIP! YIP! YIP!" Sparky
barked loudly.

Then the broomstick stopped
going upwards and started

plummeting towards the ground.

They were going to crash!

6

"Ackra-bish! Ackra-boo!
Hither, I call!
Place feathers betwixt,
so friends softly fall!"
Mrs Mothwick's voice was so loud
it made the air quiver. Sparky and

101

Carl were falling fast. *We're in for
it now!* the puppy thought as they
tumbled through the air.

Flash! A blinding golden light
filled the Courtyard. A second before
Sparky and Carl hit the ground,
a huge pile of fat feather pillows
appeared from nowhere.

They landed with a soft thud.

Phew! Sparky let out a deep sigh
of relief, but when he lifted his head,
he saw Mrs Mothwick standing over
them.

"Get up," she said sharply.

Carl scrambled upright, his hair in tangly tufts. Sparky tried to get up too, but his paws were still stuck to the broomstick.

Mrs Mothwick's eyes were steely.
She lifted her hand and said quietly:
*"Berry be stole! Beastly the trick!
Bad spell un-do! Stikwik un-stick!"*

Sparky's paws pinged free of
the broomstick. He got up slowly
with his ears drooping and his tail
between his legs.

Mr Carrion was standing by Mrs
Mothwick's feet. "As I thought," he
said coldly. "We never should have
let the dog stay—"

Sparky gave a sad whine.

"Mum, I—" Carl began, but Mrs Mothwick interrupted him.

"Mr Carrion is right," she said. "Sparky must have found a stikwik potion and used it to cheat."

Trixie was staring at Sparky, smirking. *She tricked me!* he thought, and quietly growled at her.

"The puppy *has* to go back," Mr Carrion said.

No! Sparky thought. *Please don't*

send me back to the rescue centre.

Carl's head drooped down to his chest. Mrs Mothwick lifted his chin with a long finger. "Puppies cannot be familiars, Carl," she told him. "What's more, I don't think you are ready for training quite yet."

The boy gasped, but his mum simply said, "I shall return Sparky to the rescue centre at midnight."

Sparky whimpered. *I've ruined everything*, he thought to himself.

And now I have to go back. ***I'll never see Sox or Carl again.***

"Carl's bedroom must be round here somewhere," Sparky whispered as he and Sox trotted through the dimly lit school. It was nearly bed time and they were supposed to be in the Familiars' Dormitory, but Sparky really wanted to give Carl a goodbye lick.

"That horrible Trixie should be ashamed of herself," Sox muttered.

"There!" Sparky cried as they turned a corner and entered the

Mothwick family's chambers. A
door was carved with swirly writing
which read *Carl*.

Carl's bedroom door was ajar.

Sparky pushed it with his nose.
It creaked open and he and Sox
slipped inside.

But Carl wasn't there. "I wonder
where he is," said Sox.

A light wind whispered through
the open window, blowing a sheet
of paper onto the floor.

"What's this?" Sparky held his
paw on the paper to keep it still. It
read:

I'm off to prove I AM ready for training. I've gone to the Deep Dark Wood to collect magical ingredients, just like Dad does.

Signed,

Carl Mothwick

The word "Mothwick" was underlined twice.

"Oh no!" Sparky yelped. "Mrs Mothwick said the Deep Dark Wood

is *really* dangerous. I need to find Carl!"

He sniffed the note and then the bed, until his nose was full of Carl's scent – mud and chewing gum. His claws skidded on the wood floor as he raced out of the room and down the corridor.

"Wait for me!" Sox called.

Mud and chewing gum. Mud and chewing gum.

They scampered down a wide

staircase, and out through the huge
arched doors.

"He went this way!" Sparky
barked, dashing towards the metal
school gates. Sox followed.

The gates weren't yet locked for
the night. With all his strength,
Sparky nudged one of them open.
He could see a drawbridge. Beyond
it were lots of huge trees, their
branches gently swaying.

Sox peeped round the gate too.

"Please don't go into the **Deep Dark Wood,** Sparky," the kitten said, her ears flat.

"But Carl is all by himself,"
Sparky replied, still looking at
the trees. "You stay here. Find
Mrs Mothwick and tell her what's
happened." The long shadow of the
school loomed over the Courtyard.
"I have his scent, Sox. I'll find him
quickly."

Sox gave a quiet meow and
Sparky slipped through the gap
in the gates. He bounded over the
drawbridge towards the wood.

Under the thick branches, the

ground was covered with fallen leaves. Tree roots curled up like crooked fingers. Their strange shadows seemed to be reaching out to touch Sparky as he walked. The wind in the trees sounded like someone calling his name: **"Spaaarky . . . Spaaarkeeey!"**

Sparky's nose twitched as he sniffed the air. He could still smell mud and chewing gum, but other scents whirled around him now,

too. Damp wood. Rotting leaves.
Snails. Berries. A bat.

Suddenly a strong and strange smell wafted past Sparky's nose. He'd never smelled anything like it – it was like a big cat, but also like a bird.

"A griffin!" Sparky cried, remembering what Mrs Mothwick had told them about the terrible beast. "Oh no! Carl's in even more danger than I thought."

He concentrated as hard as he could – *mud and chewing gum –*

and dashed onwards, further
and further into the **Deep
Dark
Wood.**

7

Sparky was moving quickly. He snuffled the ground and sniffed the breeze, darting left and then right, trying to follow Carl's scent.

The twilight had faded to darkness. Bright moonlight flashed

between the leaves. Sparky's paws were sore from tripping on tree roots and treading on thorny twigs, but he didn't slow down.

He reached a clearing. The smell of mud and chewing gum was now mixed with the strong scent of the griffin.

No, no! Sparky thought to himself. *Has the griffin got Carl?*

Suddenly, from high above, there came a terrible deafening

screech. Sparky quickly scrambled under a holly bush and cowered.

From his hiding place, he looked up at the sky. Silhouetted against the silver moon was a huge creature. It had a hooked beak, and sharp talons curled out from its enormous paws. Its long tail whipped from side to side. Its leathery wings beat loudly.

The griffin!

"I *have* to find Carl before the
griffin does," Sparky whispered
to himself. His nostrils flared and
he bounded on, even faster than
before. Hedgehogs scurried out of
his way as he leaped over ditches
and skidded round tree stumps.

Sparky stopped when he reached
the thick, knobbly trunk of an
ancient oak tree.

Panting heavily, he looked up
through the branches. He could see

something dangling. What was it?
A shoelace?

Sparky was afraid of making a
loud noise in case the griffin heard,
but if Carl was up the tree, he
would have to shout.

"YIP!"

The leaves rustled as Carl pushed
a branch away. His face was grubby
with mud, and twigs were tangled
in his hair. His eyes were wide and
he was shaking, but when he saw

Sparky, he grinned.

"Sparky!" Carl cried. "Good boy! How did you find me?"

Next to Carl, on a wide branch, was a massive nest made from dead branches and dry leaves. Sparky could smell that it belonged to the griffin. He whined and growled and jumped on his back legs. He didn't know how to make Carl understand. *Come on, Carl, we have to go!*

Carl swung his leg out and waved his foot around. "I've been trying to get down," he said, "but I can't!" He clung tightly to the branch.

What can I do? Sparky scampered

around the tree in desperation. On

the ground nearby he could see a
long branch. It was bendy in the
middle and had a cluster of crispy
brown leaves at one end.

It's not a broomstick, Sparky said
to himself as he ran towards it, *but it
might just do.*

Sparky chomped down hard and
let his teeth sink into the damp
wood. The branch was heavy. Weeds
had woven around it, pinning it
to the ground. Sparky heaved and

pulled until the branch was free.
Then he dragged it, little by little,
towards the enormous oak tree.

"Yif, yif!" Sparky's bark was
muffled by the wood in his mouth.

Carl looked down. "I can't play
fetch *now*," he said, looking panic-
stricken.

I need to explain, Sparky thought.
If only I could speak to him!

With Carl still watching, he
dragged the branch closer, so the

boy could see the brush of leaves at the end. Then he sat on the back.

"YIP! YIP! YIP!" he barked loudly three times. His tail wagged furiously.

Carl smiled. "Oh, I *see*," he exclaimed. "Good dog, Sparky!"

The boy pulled his wand out of his pocket. He frowned with concentration. ***Flick!*** The branch twitched at the front. ***Flick!*** The branch jerked at the back. ***Flick!*** Sparky woofed as the branch floated bumpily into the air until he was face-to-face with Carl. He dug his claws into the branch really tightly, becoming braver as he got

used to hovering above the ground.
"Wowzers! We did it!"
Carl said happily, climbing onto
the front of their bendy branch-
broomstick.

The griffin's ear-splitting screech
sounded through the trees. It was
so loud it made Sparky's ears hurt.
The branches above them began
snapping and breaking. Suddenly
an enormous talon crashed through
the leaves.

The griffin was here!

"Yip! Yip!" Sparky barked. *Let's go!*

"Ready, Sparky?" Carl cried. **"Hold on tight!"**

MRS MOTHWICK'S MAGIC ACADEMY

8

Sparky's fluffy ears waved in the
wind as he and Carl zoomed
through the woods. There was
another horrible screech, but it was
further away than before.

Sparky shivered as they passed

the last trees and left the
Deep Dark Wood. He could
see the school ahead, but the
drawbridge was up.

"We'll have to go over the wall!"
Carl shouted.

Sparky's tummy flipped as Carl
steered sharply upwards. The leaves
at the back of the bendy branch-
broomstick scraped the top of the
high wall. They made it over . . .
just.

Carl and Sparky whizzed past
the school's spiky spires. Below, in
the Courtyard, Sparky could see

Sox and the other familiars, and Mrs Mothwick pacing back and forth.

With a **bump** and a **thud**, Carl and Sparky landed in the sandpit. Sparky rolled over once, then sat up and shook the sand off his ears.

Carl sat up too. "Phew!" he said, giving Sparky a wide grin.

"There they are!" shouted Sox, and she ran over to Sparky so fast she knocked him over. "I was *so* worried."

Sparky stopped laughing when he saw Mrs Mothwick coming towards them. The other familiars were behind her.

"Carl!" Mrs Mothwick cried. She used both hands to pull Carl

up. She brushed some sand off his
jumper, then tenderly held his face
in her hands.

"You went to the **Deep Dark
Wood** *at night*?" Mrs Mothwick
said, frowning.

"I know I shouldn't have," said
Carl. "I just wanted to prove I could
be a good wizard and collect magic
ingredients . . . like Dad does . . ."
He sighed. "But I didn't find any."

Sparky rested a paw on his shoe.

"I'm just glad you are safe."
Mrs Mothwick squinted and pulled
something out of Carl's hair. It was
a long, golden feather. Her eyes

grew round. She gasped and put her
hand to her mouth.

"What is it, Mum?" Carl asked.

"A griffin's feather," Mrs
Mothwick said quietly. "Which must
mean . . . she's here!"

"Who's here?" asked Sparky.

Mrs Mothwick frowned. "Mrs
Cackleback . . ." she replied. "But
the less said about her and her
wicked ways, the better."

"Mum," said Carl, "Sparky
rescued me."

"Did he indeed?" She stooped down and looked into Sparky's eyes. His ears drooped nervously, but the witch stroked them.

"Do you remember our school motto?" Mrs Mothwick asked him. *"Fur, hand and feather, magic friends for ever.* Complete and total loyalty to your owner."

Sparky's ears pricked up and his tail wagged.

"It would seem you made a wise choice, son," Mrs Mothwick said.

"Sparky, you may have the honour of being the first puppy ever to train at our school."

"*What?!*" Trixie hissed. "Puppies aren't magical – he'll never be magical!"

Mrs Mothwick ignored Trixie and picked Sparky up. "Thank you for rescuing my son," she said softly. Then she added: "Carl, do tuck your shirt in."

Sparky licked Mrs Mothwick's knobbly nose, then scrambled into Carl's arms.

Sox purred with happiness and all the other animals

celebrated, too. Gill performed a
backflip. The rats did roly-polys.
The animals squeaked, chirped
and chattered, while Trixie
walked off with her tail in the air,
muttering, "It'll ruin this school's
reputation . . ." as she went.

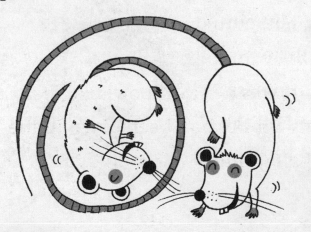

Carl plonked Sparky down on the ground. "Hang on, boy!" he said. "I've got something for you."

Sparky wagged his tail as he watched Carl run into the school. He was back in seconds. He knelt in front of Sparky and pulled something out from under his woolly jumper.

It was a brown bowl like the one Sparky had been given in the Dining Hall.

Sparky gasped as he read the
scrawly black letters written around
the side:

SPARKY

A bowl with his name on! Sparky
licked Carl all over his face.

"I don't care
if you're not
magical," Carl
said, giggling
and tickling
Sparky's

tummy. **"I think you're the best familiar ever."**

Suddenly Sparky felt tingly all over and his neck turned warm. Glancing down, he could see the bow of the shoelace Carl had tied around his neck. To his amazement,

it twinkled and glowed with a
shimmering golden light – just for a
second. Then it faded again.

Sparky barked. ***"Wowzers,
Carl! My collar glowed!"***

Carl didn't understand, but
Sparky realized it didn't matter at all.
For months he'd dreamed of a collar,
and tummy tickles, and a bowl
with his name on. *I never thought
I'd belong to a wizard*, he thought
happily, *but now I have an owner!*

Sparky nuzzled Carl and knew that, magic or no magic, he had everything he had ever wanted.

Turn over to read a sneak peek of the next

book in this series, **SPARKY'S BAD SPELL!**

MRS MOTHWICK'S MAGIC ACADEMY

1

Sparky stood beside his wizard, Carl, trying to keep still. He hadn't been at Mrs Mothwick's Magic Academy for long, but he'd already seen most of the training rooms and this one was his favourite.

The wallpaper was dark crimson with a swirly gold pattern, and the windows stretched from the floor to the ceiling. Each one was draped with heavy, red velvet curtains. They smelled old.

"Settle down now, please," said the teacher, Mr Noble, peering over his rectangular glasses.

All around Sparky, the familiars fidgeted nervously next to their owners – apart from an upside-

down bat, who swung from his witch's fingertip.

Over the **squawks** and **squeaks** of the birds and animals, Mr Noble tried again: "Welcome to Beginners' Magic Class." He puffed out his plump, rosy cheeks. "It's now time for you all to demonstrate your tricks."

Sparky's tail wagged. He pawed Carl's shoe, and the boy glanced down and gave him a wink.

"Have you done your homework, Sox?" Sparky whispered to his best friend, who was sitting next to him.

Sox was a black kitten with white paws that looked like socks. "Yes, we have a trick," she replied, with one ear flattening a little. "But I'm not sure we've practised enough . . ."

Sox's witch, Sophie, bent down and her long hair flopped forward and tickled Sparky's nose.

"What's Sparky saying to you?"

Sophie whispered to Sox.

"He wondered," Sox replied, "whether we'd done our homework and—"

"Sshhh!" came a hiss from behind them.

Sparky turned to see Trixie glaring at them. Her witch, Amelia, flicked her perfect black ponytail snootily. Trixie's perfect black tail swished in time.

They turned to look at Mr Noble

as he started speaking.

"The purpose of the homework," he said thoughtfully, "was to see how you familiars and witches and wizards work together. As we all know: **A witch is not a witch without a familiar, and a familiar is not a familiar without a witch**."

Every witch and wizard needed a familiar — an animal to help them

do magic. Sparky was so happy
that he was Carl's familiar . . . even
though he wasn't much help when
it came to magic! But he and Carl
had been practising their trick all
week. They definitely wouldn't be
bottom of the class this time.

"By now," Mr Noble continued,
"I expect most of you are managing
to communicate with each other
with a few words."

Sparky's ears drooped. He still

hadn't managed to say a single word that Carl could understand.

"Joshua and Finley," Mr Noble said to a wizard and his ferret familiar. "Why don't you go first with your trick?"

Finley stood on his back legs, looked at Joshua, and squeaked.

"Dook-dook-dook!"

Joshua shrugged, a worried expression on his face. He couldn't

understand what his familiar was
saying.

Some of the witches giggled.

The ferret frowned in
concentration and tried again.

"Dook . . . din . . . s-s-spin!"
he finally squeaked.

Joshua flicked his wand towards
his shoes, creating a cloud of glitter.
Finley began running in a circle
around his feet. The boy stood on

his tiptoes. All the witches leaned
forward to watch as Joshua began

to spin. He went faster and faster, until he and Finley were just a blur.

"S-s-s-stop!" squeaked Finley.

"Yes! Please stop!" Joshua shouted. Finley stopped running, and Joshua, looking very dizzy, slowly came to a halt. Everyone clapped as they staggered back to their places.

"Very good," Mr Noble said. "A slow start, Finley, but you got there in the end with your words. Well done." He looked around the room. "Now let's see Trixie and Amelia."

"Finally," Trixie muttered as they

pushed past Sparky.

When everyone was quiet, Trixie purred: "Allow me to introduce Amelia, the great-great-granddaughter of Madame Marvella, inventor of a thousand potions."

Sparky's heart did an extra beat when he saw how expert Trixie had become at talking to her witch.

Amelia smiled. "Thank you, Trixie. And allow me to introduce

Trixie, one of seventeen generations of feline familiars."

"They're so good at communicating," Sparky whispered.

"They're so good at being show-offs!" Sox replied.

Amelia flicked her wand and a golden orb of light floated into the air. Trixie twitched her shiny whiskers. A glittery spark appeared and shot towards the orb.

There was a ***flash!***

Then, **_Bang! Pop! Whizz!_**

Bright green and gold fireworks began exploding above the heads of all the trainees and familiars. Three white mice, Harry, Larry and Sid, squealed and jumped into their wizards' pockets to hide.

"Thank you, Trixie and Amelia," Mr Noble yelled above the noise. "That's enough now."

Everyone clapped as Trixie and Amelia made their way back to

their places, beaming smugly.

"Ah, er . . . Sparky and Carl!" Mr Noble called.

Sparky's tummy flipped. *This is it!*

At the front of the class, Carl took out his slightly bent wand. "Ready?" he asked Sparky.

The pup shuffled on his paws and wagged his tail. "Yip!" he replied. *I'm ready!*

"My wonderful puppy Sparky and I would like to show you our

amazing tricks," Carl said in a
booming voice.

All the trainees grew silent.

Carl held his wand above
Sparky's head. "Sit!" he said.

Sparky immediately sat on his
bottom. He wagged his tail.

"Play dead!" Carl said.

Sparky rolled onto his back and
let his tongue flop out of the side
of his mouth. He heard someone
sniggering.

Carl fumbled in his pocket and brought out a red rubber ball. Sparky sat up straight and waited.

"Fetch!" Carl yelled as he threw the ball across the room.

Sparky was off like a dart. He caught the ball in his mouth mid-bounce, then scrambled back across the wooden floor and dropped it at Carl's feet.

Carl grinned, scooped up the

ball, then turned to everyone watching. "Ta-da!"

The whole room went silent for a moment. Then everyone erupted into laughter. Sparky's tail drooped between his legs.

"**Quiet!**" Mr Noble shouted. His face was usually kind, but now it looked very stern. "Everyone be quiet."

The class settled down again.

"Carl," Mr Noble said softly. "I

can see that you and Sparky have a
very strong bond."

Carl's cheeks were bright red
now. He stared at the floor.

"It's just . . ." Mr Noble paused.
"We really need to start seeing you
do some . . . magic."

Carl sighed.

Sparky whined.

Mrs Mothwick's Magic Academy
had never allowed a puppy in
before. Everyone seemed to think

puppies didn't make good familiars. But Sparky really thought they'd done well this time. Now it seemed that poor Carl was going to get the lowest mark – again.

All because Sparky wasn't magical.

What Animal Is Your Familiar?

Take this brilliant quiz to find out!

1. How do you like to spend your spare time?

A) Playing with my best friends

B) Reading books or writing my own stories

C) Playing football with my friends

D) Drawing or making things

E) Going to the park

2. What is your favourite subject at school?

A) Maths

B) English

C) Sports

D) Art

E) Science

3. What is your bedroom like?

A) I try to keep it tidy, but sometimes I forget

to put things away

B) My room is nice and quiet

C) I have lots of pictures and posters on the walls

D) My room is so messy I can't find anything

E) My room is full of traps to keep my family out!

4. Which magical power would you most

like to have?

A) Invisibility

B) Flight

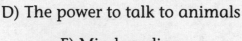

C) Super strength

D) The power to talk to animals

E) Mind reading

5. What do you find most annoying?

A) Not being allowed to stay up late

B) People who are mean or rude to others

C) Having to do homework

D) Being told what to do

E) Getting into trouble when I haven't done

anything wrong

6. What is your favourite colour?

A) Purple

B) Black

C) Red

D) Blue

E) Orange

7. If your friend was going to do something they shouldn't, what would you do?

A) Tell them it's a bad idea but let them do it anyway

B) Ask them why they wanted to do it and think of something better to do

C) Join them. It might be fun and if we get caught we can take the blame together

D) Persuade them not to do it

E) Threaten to tell a grown-up

8. Which word do you think describes you best?

A) Friendly

B) Quiet

C) Adventurous

D) Creative

E) Hardworking

Results:

Mostly As: Your familiar is a cat!

Mostly Bs: Your familiar is an owl!

Mostly Cs: Your familiar is a rat!

Mostly Ds: Your familiar is a squirrel!

Mostly Es: Your familiar is a frog!

A bit of a mix: Your familiar isn't one of the usual animals. But, as Sparky and Carl are finding out, there might be a little bit of magic in other animals, too . . . or maybe your familiar is a mythical creature like Mrs Cackleback's griffin (but much friendlier, of course!).

Spot the Difference

There are five differences between these two pictures.

Can you find them all?

Turn to the back of the book to see the answers!

Witchy Wordsearch

Ten words are hidden in the wordsearch.

Can you find them all?

G	S	S	G	W	T	H	J	K	A	X
R	C	P	R	M	I	M	F	P	Z	F
I	B	A	I	H	J	T	O	L	H	A
F	Q	R	H	D	A	Y	C	I	I	M
F	D	K	Y	F	E	M	B	H	C	I
I	Z	Y	I	A	E	R	C	A	R	L
N	D	Z	V	M	A	G	I	C	E	I
G	E	N	A	M	T	S	F	J	K	A
Z	H	T	R	I	X	I	E	H	W	R
B	Y	W	I	N	O	G	A	C	O	T
B	R	O	O	M	S	T	I	C	K	D

1. Sparky

2. Carl

3. Magic

4. Familiar

5. Sox

6. Trixie

7. Broomstick

8. Griffin

9. Witch

10. Spider

Turn to the back of the book to see the answers!

Trixie's Tricky Quiz

1. Where did Sparky and Sox live before they were taken to Mrs Mothwick's Magic Academy?
2. What kind of animal is Mr Carrion?
3. What does Sparky think Carl smells of?
4. What are the names of the three white mice?
5. What is the academy's motto?
6. Who persuaded Sparky to pick the stikwik berry?

Turn to the back of the book to see the answers!

Amelia's Amazing Anagrams

Can you unscramble these words and match them

to the correct answer?

Ark Spy	Familiar
Gawky Mismatch	Marshmallows
Cosmic DreamFear	
	Mr Carrion
Ah Small Worms	Sparky
Skirt Combo	Mrs Mothwick's
Can Mirror	Magic Academy
If I Alarm	Broomstick

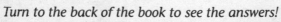

Turn to the back of the book to see the answers!

Magical Leads

Can you work out which young witch or wizard has been paired with each familiar?

Joe

Justin

Polly

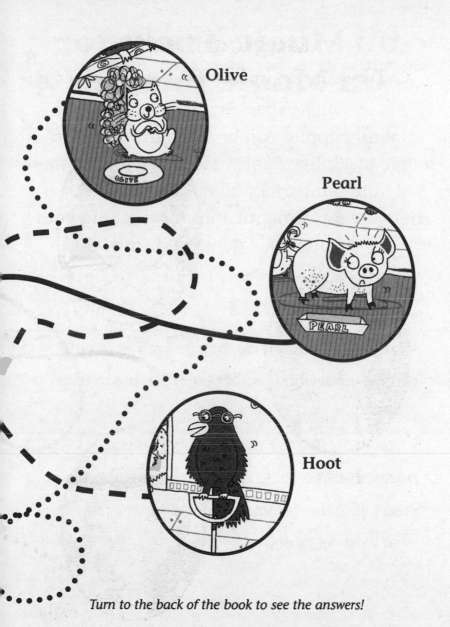

Olive

Pearl

Hoot

Turn to the back of the book to see the answers!

Un-Magic Tricks for
Un-Magic Puppies

Not all puppies can be familiars and learn magic tricks, like Sparky is hoping to. But there are some tricks all dogs can learn.
Here are some instructions for teaching your dog to sit, lie down and crawl.

You will need:

• A dog

• A lot of patience (it might take your dog a little while to understand what you are trying to teach him!)

• Dog treats (try to find something your dog really likes. You could try using dog biscuits or small pieces of cheese or ham – some dogs even like vegetables!)

Sit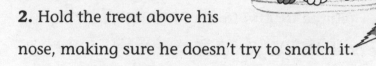

1. Get your dog to stand in front of you and show him the treat in your hand.

2. Hold the treat above his nose, making sure he doesn't try to snatch it.

3. Slowly move the treat towards the back of his head.

4. Your dog will sit down as he follows the treat with his eyes and nose.

5. Say "Sit" and give him the treat.

You will have to do this quite a few times, but eventually your dog will know the command "Sit". Make sure you always reward your dog for following a command, either with a treat, a stroke or by saying "Good dog".

Lie Down ⭐

1. Using the command "Sit", get your dog to sit down in front of you.

2. Hold the treat in front of his nose, making sure he doesn't try to snatch it.

3. Say "Down" and slowly move the treat towards the floor.

4. Your dog will follow the treat with his eyes and nose.

5. When your dog's nose is on the ground, slowly drag the treat across the floor towards you.

6. Your dog will lie down as he follows the treat with his eyes and nose.

7. Say "Down" and give him the treat.

You will have to do this quite a few times, but eventually your dog will know the command "Down". Make sure you always reward your dog for following a command, either with a treat, a stroke or by saying "Good dog".

Crawl

1. Using the command "Down", get your dog to lie down in front of you.

2. Hold the treat in front of his nose, making sure he doesn't try to snatch it.

3. Keep one hand gently over his back and slowly move the treat along the floor in a line.

4. Your dog will follow the treat along the floor.

5. Say "Crawl" and give him the treat.

You will have to do this quite a few times, but eventually your dog will know the command "Crawl". Make sure you always reward your dog for following a command, either with a treat, a stroke or by saying "Good dog".

Answers

Spot the Difference

Trixie's Tricky Quiz:

1. Green Meadow Rescue Centre
2. A vulture
3. Mud and chewing gum
4. Harry, Larry and Sid
5. "Hand, fur and feather, magic friends for ever!"
6. Trixie

Amelia's Amazing Anagrams

Ark Spy is *Sparky*; Gawky Mismatch Cosmic Dream is *Mrs Mothwick's Magic Academy*; Ah Small Worms is *Marshmallows*; Skirt Combo is *Broomstick*; If I Alarm is *Familiar*; Can Mirror is *Mr Carrion*

Witchy Wordsearch

G	S	S	G	W	T	H	J	K	A	X
R	C	P	R	M	I	M	F	P	Z	F
I	B	A	I	H	J	T	O	L	H	A
F	Q	R	H	D	A	Y	C	I	I	M
F	D	K	Y	F	E	M	B	H	C	I
I	Z	Y	I	A	E	R	C	A	R	L
N	D	Z	V	M	A	G	I	C	E	I
G	E	N	A	M	T	S	F	J	K	A
Z	H	T	R	I	X	I	E	H	W	R
B	Y	W	I	N	O	G	A	C	O	T
B	R	O	O	M	S	T	I	C	K	D

Magical Leads

Joe is paired with Hoot.

Justin is paired with Pearl.

Polly is paired with Olive.